Needle in a Haystack

extracts from the diary of Charlie Duke

Charlie begins her third year at secondary school with the bullying reaching its peak and no one to turn to. How will she get through another year of being the only disabled student at a main stream school?

This is a pivotal point in a young girl's life, with family tragedy, new friendships and the first glimpse of romance. We are plunged deeply into the mind of Charlie Duke as we read extracts from her personal diary. Needle In a Haystack takes us on a journey through the early twists and turns that build our inner strength.

Needle in a Haystack is Sally's second novel. To find out more about Charlie Duke, read 'How to Love'.

Needle in a Haystack

extracts from the diary of
Charlie Duke

Sally Edwards

First published in Great Britain in 2016 by

Figtree Industries

3 Prospect Cottages

Snailbeach

Shrewsbury

SY5 0LR

A CIP catalogue record of this book is available from the British Library

This novel is entirely a work of fiction.
The characters and incidents portrayed in it are a work of the author's imagination.

ISBN 978-0-9572390-5-0

Designed and typeset in Sandscript by Figtree Industries
Cover photograph by Silvia Sala
Produced by Figtree Industries

Needle in a Haystack

Friday October 1st

Dear Diary, I don't normally do these sorts of things, it's a bit too girly for me, and as everyone knows, I'm not the fluffy girly type. But I have recently started my third year at secondary school and the nasty stuff hasn't stopped. No one else would believe me if I told them anyway, so you are my only friend.

I know you won't make fun and tell the whole school my secrets – what I tell you will go no further.

Bearing in mind I don't even have any friends in school you won't be surprised to learn that there's no boyfriend yet, either. Besides, the boys in my school are so disgusting and they are only interested in football...

A re-run of Happy Days started tonight and I love it! The Fonz is so cool; Dad even calls me Fonz, I watch it so much. Hmm, I wonder how much a leather jacket costs? I would love one just like Fonz. I don't want the goth look, like the other girls, but a leather jacket just like

Fonz - yeah! I know mum won't let me, though, she won't even let me go to youth club, so no wonder I have no friends.

My classmates (I shall call them 'the Goths') must have broken a world record today - it only took them thirty seconds in registration to snap a rude comment towards me and my new haircut. I can't tell Mum because she did it for me in the holidays and it would really upset her. I hate the way the girls speak to me and make fun, but they are the coolest girls in school and I wish I was popular like them - maybe one day. Perhaps I will make head girl, or maybe things will never change in this awful place I'm forced to go to for five miserable days of the week. Trying to find someone prepared to be my friend is like trying to find a needle in a haystack. So, yes, the name calling, sniggering and rude comments continue into a new term. I'm so sick of all this; why can't everyone just be friends like they were in special school? I had so many really good friends in school, it's a shame some of them couldn't come here with me. I miss them – we had so much fun. I probably won't see them ever again, but I have been told going to normal school will be "good for me", so here I am.

Mum's calling for me to turn off my light for bed, so I will write again in a few days.

Monday October 8th

Hello it's me...of course! I must give you a name - can't keep calling you Diary. Or will that make me look crazy? But Diary doesn't seem right.

I had the most amazing weekend. Mum and Dad and my little sister, Dylan, came with me to Rhyl on a Sunday school trip. I know I'm getting too old, but all the other girls from the singing group go and it's always good fun. I get to sit on the back seat of the bus. I'm allowed because... well Grandad owns the company, so it's fine!

We sang some group songs and our favourite pop songs, shared sandwiches and crisps and had a right good laugh. Mum let us have fish and chips for tea, looking out across the waves. I love the sea, and hearing the waves keeps me calm. I'm not sleeping too well at the moment: the bullying from the Goths is getting worse. Today, the spiteful lot voted me as form captain, to make a show of me, so teacher's pet is the new name I've been given, on top of the rest. I think Mum and Dad wanted to cheer me up. I know they are having problems, too; I heard them arguing again the other night – I hope it's nothing serious. Louise's mum and dad divorced last year and she was really upset by it. I'm a bit worried this will happen with Mum and Dad and my family will be split up.

I start drama at school next Monday, and I'm quite excited. I like singing in groups, so I hope this is going to be as much fun. Besides, I like Mr Ashley; he is head of year and keeps a close eye on things for me. He seems to be quite approachable but I've heard him yell at a few kids and I definitely wouldn't like to be told off by him – he is very loud. Who knows, I might like this drama business and get a part in the end of term production, but that means being friends with the others so I doubt that will actually happen. I will let you know how it goes.

I have Geography homework tonight and it's hard so I need to study, but I will write and let you know how drama class goes... that's if my house doesn't get blown up. There is still a war going on in Iraq. Mum is always freaking out and thinks we are all going to die, and Grandad keeps telling me stories of when he was an RAF engineer in WW2.

Monday October 25th

I'm furious! Why can't they see I'm just the same as them? We had drama and it was quite good fun. There were some warm-up games at first, then later we had to get into pairs, which is when the trouble started. No one wanted to pair with me, so I was left with no option but to work with Emily, who also struggled to find a partner. She's okay, I guess, but very slow and speaks a bit odd. She's new to the school; her younger brother is here too; they both have white blond hair and are very skinny. Emily is really tall too, which makes her look even skinnier. I avoided her at first, but we actually got on quite well. She's shy but is very funny and said some really funny things about the Goths. It seems she's another of their victims, so we have something in common. She even asked to meet at lunchtime, which has never happened before. She told me all about how she finds it hard making friends. Her dad is in the Air Force and gets moved around a lot, so she keeps moving school. She is originally from Hampshire, which I learned from my Geography homework is near London. She speaks funny and it makes me laugh. She says things like "larf" instead of laff and "Barth" instead of Bath, which is another thing the Goths pick up on. We found the drama workshop quite hard but okay. At least she didn't make fun of me. And Mr Ashley said I made a really good effort in class. I just wish he hadn't mentioned it in front of the rest, though.

I have decided not to watch Newsround anymore because they keep talking about what's happening over in Iraq and it really scares me.

It looks like the Goths are having problems: two of the girls have got boyfriends they want to spend time with at school, and the others don't like it. I wonder what the boys see in them, anyway? They are spiteful, loud and always in trouble. I quite like Laura's hair though; she's the prettiest of them all and even wears makeup. She looks like a model.

Mum and Dad seem to be okay at the moment. I know dad is working hard, but we do spend lots of time together, especially at the weekend, when Mum is busy looking after my little sister. We went kite

flying in the fields over by our house
today; it was windy so the kite flew
really well – I couldn't hold onto it
for long but Dad was great and said
I was getting the hang of it. I was
doing fine until we went down the
field a bit further, only to find we
were sharing it with not a large cow
but one of the farmer's bulls, which
looked very annoyed when it
spotted us. Dad dropped the kite on
the ground, picked me up in one arm
and my wheelchair in another, and
we ran home like lightning. Mum
wasn't too impressed by our
adventure, saying we shouldn't have
been there in the first place, but
Dad and I just couldn't stop

laughing. That bull was really mad at us – we were very lucky.

I am having lunch with Emily, again, at school tomorrow. She sits next to me in history now, so it finally feels like I have a friend in school. No matter how much I try to get into the Goths' good books they just keep making fun or ignoring me.

Next week, in school, we are doing lots to raise money for Sport Relief, which supports good causes. I've decided to be brave and do something of my own to help. I'm doing a sponsored walk around the school playground on Friday lunchtime, in my callipers. I hate being in them at school, but if I can do something useful for others, then why not? So I'm busy making sponsor forms. My family and neighbours have sponsored me, so I've already been promised lots of money. I don't think the kids at school will give anything, but hopefully some of the staff will. I just hope that no one will do what Adam did at special school and creep up behind me and put grass cuttings down my back, or else pull me over so I'm laying on my back without being able to get up... I never spoke to him ever again after that and I made sure he got into trouble for it. I can't let these fears stop me from doing it, though. Emily says she will keep me company and stop people giving me a hard time.

Dad says if the weather is going to be good next Saturday I can go with him on the bus to his away football game. He isn't as good as his West Ham heroes but he always plays, so the manager must think he is quite good. Dad keeps saying he is getting too old, so he has decided to take up golf just in case he has to stop playing. Mum wasn't too impressed by this and it caused another big argument. She said it was just another excuse to go drinking. Dad argued back that it is his time to be with the lads, just like she spends time with her girlfriends going to concerts and coffee mornings that normally last well into the afternoon... I think Dad's got a point.

Sunday November 2nd

Dear Silent One, sorry I haven't written anything for a while; things have been really bad. Worst of all, there was the awful day at school known as Sport Relief Day, which turned out to be the perfect excuse for the Goths to turn up the heat on me. They followed me round for most of my sponsored walk, calling me names and laughing at me, saying stuff like: "Hope the wind doesn't get rough, it might blow you over," and "Look at the bionic kid over there with her metal legs." They only disappeared because Mr Ashley made an appearance. He was really good; he actually gave me loads of encouragement – said I set a good example and that the school should be proud of me. I think, at one point, I saw him wipe away a tear.

Sunday December 12th

My whole world got turned upside down two days ago. Mum and Dad sat me down and told me things were not working out and that dad was moving out of the house. Things at work are getting worse and he's losing more money than he's making. I think he has been drinking more, and I have heard them shouting at each other more than ever. I can't believe it has come to this. Dad is the one I can always talk to about stuff and now he is gone. He has moved back in with Nan and my step-grandad, over twenty miles away, so I don't think I will be seeing much of him for a while. Mum says it's final and that she is going for divorce. With this, and the Goths giving me a hard time, I don't think I have ever felt so lonely and upset. I got really angry and tearful last night - not sure what happened but I woke up with a badly cut hand. The pain from my knuckles was so bad I had forgotten all about Mum and Dad for a few minutes; then Mum came

into my room and I remembered all
over again. I keep asking her if she
thinks there's any chance she and
Dad will get back together, but she
is determined they won't. I feel so
lost; it's like he died or something.
How am I going to get over this one?
Now he is gone, and Mum spends
her time looking after my little
sister, you really are the only one I
can tell my feelings to. I don't trust
anyone at school. I hope I feel
better soon. I hate my life.

Sunday January 16th

I don't seem to have much time to write to you these days. I'm seeing more of Dad. He takes me out at weekends, so I always enjoy my Saturday. I have exams coming up so I'm studying every night. I find it so hard to remember what I'm learning, I just can't keep all the information in my head, but if I ask for help and the idiots find out, I will be a total laughing stock, so I'm struggling to cope on my own. I thought Laura and Debs were beginning to like me - they speak to me in form more, and they even offered to help me at lunch the other day, but I should have known better. I was doing my usual solo circuit round the outside playground - Emily was sick, so I was Billy-no-mates. Laura had been borrowing my pens and ruler in maths and was quite chatty, but when I got to the corner of science block I heard voices and laughing. It was Laura and the others and they were obviously talking about me. They were calling my chair a buggy and I heard Debs make fun of my little legs – calling me rubber legs. At this I turned the corner, looked straight at them, said hello and turned right back around and went as far down the playground as fast as I could, leaving them with embarrassed faces. How could they be so nice to me one minute, then call me horrible names the next? What is so wrong with me that has made them hate me so much?

After dinner that night, I stayed in my room listening to music, trying to cheer myself up, but not even my beloved Take That could make me smile. I lay down and all I could hear was the laughter of the Goths and everything they said about me.

I burst into tears and buried my head in my pillow. I turned onto my side and something stuck into my rib cage. Looking down, I saw it was my hair dryer. At this point I was so mad I picked it up and threw it against the wall, smashing the end off the plug. I slammed my wardrobe door shut, trapping my thumb. The pain was so bad I thought I would lose my thumb. I stuck my fingers in my mouth, suddenly realising I was in so much pain that I had forgotten what I was angry about. Mum came into my room, having heard a noise, so I told her something had fallen off the top of my wardrobe and I was trying to lift it. The force of me slamming the wardrobe door was so bad that an old photo album had actually fallen on the floor, so I got away with my little white lie. After Mum left, I picked up the photo album and opened it. Old photos of me as a baby, being held by Dad, stared right back at me. My heart sank and tears began to run down my cheeks. I quickly put the book away and looked up at my bedroom wall and felt myself smile again as I studied the poster of Robbie Williams. I got back into my bed and played the Take That album one last time before settling down for the night. Just as I was about to close my eyes, I felt a warm trickling sensation on my little finger; I was bleeding. I had cut my finger on a broken piece of plug, which I had smashed in my rage. I found this strangely amusing, realising that whenever I hurt myself I don't feel sad or angry anymore. I sucked the blood away, closed my eyes and fell asleep.

Monday January 24th

It's getting colder, Silent One. The only thing I like about this time of year is the fact it's my birthday in two weeks and mum says I can go to see some old friends from where I used to live before we bought the business. They were my real friends because they knew me as a small child. They grew up and accepted my disability and treated me just like anyone should do, unlike those hateful girls at the school I go to now. If the school nearer home had been more accessible I should have gone there, but they put me in this place instead so I'm stuck with it. Some good things have happened at school, though, since I last wrote. My maths exam results were so bad the Head of Department told me they won't be entering me for a final exam in that subject. And because they have decided that carrying me upstairs to science is too dangerous, I get extra private lessons downstairs. Work has even begun on a new accessible toilet and changing room, just for me, which makes me feel quite special. Laura got into a big fight at school and is now suspended for a week, so I get some peace and quiet at last... funny how she starts the trouble and the rest follow. I might actually get some proper studying done now she's not around. Even Mr Ashley said I seemed different today. His drama lesson was good; I'm still only working with Emily, but she's great fun and sticks up for me at times. I'm getting better marks than the others, so it's their loss, not mine. I wonder what Dad will get me for my birthday? Mum said I could have my ears pierced; I hope it doesn't hurt.

Laura always wears nice earrings,
so I can get some nice ones, too,
after my birthday.

Wednesday February 2nd

So, that was the week from Hell.
The toilet room at school is finished
in record time and has very quickly
been christened "the cell", by who
else? Yes, Laura. She is back from
suspension, and don't I know it? My
best friend from the village has
come down with mumps so won't be
coming for my birthday. Dad came

round today with my present; he
was trying to act all mysterious, but
it's obviously a guitar - bless him, he
still thinks I'm eight. Mum had a go
at him because she hasn't received
any money from him for a couple of
months, but he is struggling to come
to terms with only earning a small
wage, since losing the business and
having to work for someone else. He
has been looking for a flat and has
just been to sign for one in the
town. It's only tiny, he says, but big
enough just for him. He can't afford
anything bigger. I know mum is
struggling with me and my sister,
but he's struggling too and she just
keeps yelling at him. I came home
from school and whizzed through

the door all excited because his car was outside, only to run in on a massive argument. Mum eventually kicked him out and started crying. She said some really horrible things about dad that made me cry, too. A new P.E Teacher started at school today - Miss Brady. She seems too young to be a teacher. She's all enthusiastic and happy; I told her *that* won't last long. She's got a sense of humour, which makes a nice change from all the other fossils in school. She says she is going to create a new P.E. routine for me as I've been excluded from taking part so far; so we will see what bright ideas she comes up with. She actually stood up for me today and argued that I had every right to get P.E. lessons, so she's feisty... She wears nice perfume, too; I wonder why her hair is so short? She looks almost like a boy from the back, but she's very pretty.

Watch this space! I could become an Olympic champion yet, if she has her way. So she tells me.

Until next time, Silent One... I hope Mum and Dad stop fighting soon.

Monday February 7th

I feel so sick! Today is my birthday
but I have been awake all night,
crying. The phone rang very late
last night and as mum was talking I
could hear her start to cry. I knew
something was very wrong. Minutes
later, my bedroom door opened and
mum came to sit on my bed as I
turned on the light to see what was

wrong. It was the local police station, asking if Mum knew my dad's new address. A police officer had to break into a flat in town after suspicions were raised over a man not turning up for work for a few days and neighbours not seeing him leave the house or draw the curtains. Mum confirmed it was Dad's flat... Dad was dead, and had been for about three days, according to the coroner. They may have been separated, but Mum was still so upset. Words cannot describe how I feel; I can't stop crying! I just cannot believe I will never see Dad again; he was my dad; he was special; he was my hero. Even though things went bad

for us as a family, I still loved him.
How could I not love Dad? Mum rang
school and told them, and they
have given me a few days off. I've
got cards and presents here, on my
bed, to open, but all I want is for
my dad to walk through the door. I
know it won't ever happen again. I
don't know how I will ever sleep,
because I'm scared that if I close
my eyes I will forget what he looked
like or how his voice sounded. Mum is
trying to be strong, for the sake of
me and my sister, but they were
married a long time and I know she
is upset. Why did this have to
happen, just before my birthday? I
don't want to celebrate my
birthday, ever again. I can't even

see Emily for a few days; she's my only friend in school, so I have absolutely no one to talk to. I want to go to sleep and never wake up; I want my dad back! I HATE MY LIFE! Happy Birthday, Charlotte. Yeah, thanks a lot.

Friday March 18th

How long is it supposed to take to get over someone dying? Everyone around me seems to have picked up their lives and gone back to normal but I'm still having nightmares and waking up in tears. I can't tell anyone – I'm meant to be "over it", by now. My day at school was pretty good, though; I've been

working hard on some games and
fitness ideas with Miss Brady. We
even played a kind of basket
ball/netball type game from my
wheelchair. She borrowed one from
sick bay and tried it herself, and I
couldn't stop laughing when she
tipped it up and fell backwards. I
am used to all that, but she was
really shocked. After class, she told
me about a youth club she runs in
the village next to where I live. She's
had her hair cut very short, but it's
nice. I don't think she has a
boyfriend or is married; she hasn't
got a ring on her finger. I wonder
why not? She's very pretty and
very funny; she makes me laugh.
She's invited me to her youth club,

but mum won't let me go. It's so
unfair; she says there's no-one to
look after me, but Miss Brady would
be there. I wish Mum would treat
me the same as the others get
treated; I feel like a baby
sometimes. I hate it!
I'm beginning to look forward to my
P.E. lessons each week; we have fun
and Miss Brady says I'm getting
really good at the games she's
giving me. I can walk further, now,
in my callipers, without getting
tired, so I must be getting better. I
wish I had a friend in school like
Miss Brady, she's funny. She talks
to me like a grown-up and says nice
things to me. My hair is getting on
my nerves; it's growing so quick. I'm

going to ask mum to cut it soon – but cut it shorter than she normally does, a bit like Miss Brady's. She's so stylish; I wonder what she wears when she's not in school? Mum asked me, today, if I had a boyfriend, or if I liked anyone. I hate the boys; I just like having my lesson with Miss Brady. She's the best bit about school, now, for definite. I spoke to her about being sad about my dad and she seemed to really understand. She even said that if I ever needed to talk to anyone, she would like to help, which I thought was so lovely. But I'm not surprised; she's the best... I wonder what her name is? She said that, next lesson, she would let me into a secret which might help me. I wonder what that is? I can't wait for next week. Tomorrow, I'm going to ask mum to cut my hair — I hope she will.

Monday March 21st

Had the best time with Emily,
today; she's so funny. I told her I
wanted my hair cut, so she brought
in some of her mum's magazines, so
we could choose a style. She told me
all about her brother getting into
trouble on a skiing trip with school,
which reminded me of a funny story
from special school. We laughed so

much about it, she nearly wet herself. We looked through the magazine but I couldn't find any style I liked. Then, just at the end of break, Miss Brady went past and I pointed her out to Emily, and said, "That's the hair I want." She heard me, and stopped and turned around, and said, "You can't have it, it's mine." We all laughed as she walked away.

I told Emily the story of a weekend trip to Wales, with my class. One day we visited a beach. I was being pushed, in my wheelchair, by Mrs Jones, down towards the water's edge, when she whispered in my ear, "I'm going to push you to the edge and leave you there." We both laughed, but, as we got nearer, she started to run really fast. I was scared she was actually going to leave me there, stuck in the soft sand. I really thought this was going to happen, so just as she reached the bottom I slammed on my wheelchair brakes to stop her from going any further. But my front wheels got stuck in the wet sand and sunk, which tipped my chair forward. The force of this made Mrs Jones fall forward, over my chair, and she landed in a heap on the sand in front of me. She didn't speak to me all the way back to our cottage that day, but my friends thought it was very funny.

By the time school finished, I had chosen my hair style, and asked mum about it when I got home. She wasn't too keen, but agreed eventually, mumbling to herself something about it growing back fast anyway.

Monday March 21st

Something strange happened after school tonight. Mum was watching a film called Boys Don't Cry, as I was getting ready for bed, and there was this bit where two ladies were kissing... not a peck on the cheek, but *really* kissing. And one looked like a boy – short hair, jeans and a leather jacket just like the one I want. I was shocked, but I had a strange nice feeling afterwards. What did it mean? I haven't seen this before. Do girls kiss girls? Do boys kiss boys? Euh, imagine Alex and Steven kissing! But they seemed happy on the film; it was sweet. I wonder if Miss Brady has kissed a girl, ever? Does she know what all that means? I might ask her; she's very clever; I'm sure she will know.

Tuesday March 22nd

I'm not sure if I dare tell Emily this,
but I had a strange dream last
night. I dreamed I was in the local
park with Emily, one day, listening
to music and reading our Shout
magazines, and swapping posters,
when Miss Brady came by and
started to talk to us. She wasn't in
school clothes; she was all dressed

up – going out for a night somewhere – and she looked really good. She was all smiles, and happy, and hung out with us, sitting next to me for ages. I think she was flirting with me. I woke up with such a huge smile on my face. Should I tell Emily, or not? I'm confused. What does this mean? I won't tell Emily today. I have P.E. tomorrow, so I'm all excited to see Miss Brady. She said she had a secret to tell me. I wonder what it is?

Friday March 25th

So, school was amazing today. I got a grade A for my English essay, which was a good start, then I had double P.E. this afternoon. Miss Brady told me a little about herself. Before becoming a teacher she was in the Army, based first in Northern Ireland, then was one of the first soldiers to go into Bosnia.

She joined the Intelligence Corps in the Gulf before she retired. She told me she was injured quite badly during an attack, leaving nasty scars on her back, from debris, that stopped her from running over long distances or carrying kit. Plus, she was badly affected by what she witnessed. Emotionally, she suffers from something called PTSD. She has nightmares, can't stand loud bangs, and gets very depressed. She even told me she's tried to kill herself. I can't believe that someone who seems so happy around school is so unhappy and full of suffering.

A lot of what she told me made me think about how I feel

sometimes about being bullied at school, and about Dad dying. I think she was trying to tell me she understands a lot about what I'm feeling, which is so nice of her. She is the best.

Tuesday April 26th

Hello Silent One. Mum finally gave
in and has cut my hair short
exactly the way I want it this time
– I love it. She took me shopping on
Saturday. With my birthday money
I bought some DVDs and a leather
jacket; not quite the same as The
Fonz, but almost... Dad would love it!
When I got home from school,

earlier, mum told me she had a
letter from school. It was from Miss
Brady, telling Mum about the youth
club she runs and saying how much
she thinks I would enjoy it. Mum
said, "Okay, you can go one week
and see how you like it and then we
will see, after that." So we are
going to McDonald's for tea then
she's dropping me off and picking
me up later. It's not until Thursday
but I can't wait.

She said, "I need to fatten you up,
you have lost weight, young lady."
I've been keeping a big secret; I
can't eat anything properly. I have
my tea then I go and throw it all
back up. I've not had lunch at
school for about a week, either. I'm

just never hungry and the smell of food is making me feel sick. I don't know why, but I just can't eat, and now Mum has seen I have lost weight! I've also picked a really big scab on my elbow and made it bleed, but it happened before I knew what I was doing. When I did it I didn't feel sad anymore. Why do I like to hurt myself? And why can't I eat?

Thursday April 28th

At last, today was Thursday!
School was a drag. Laura was a
total pain in History, again. I
wonder why she plays up and gets
herself into so much trouble? She
even got me into trouble for talking
in Maths. I was so mad.
Anyway, I went to that youth
group Miss Brady invited me to.

Mum took me for a McDonald's first and gave me a huge lecture about how to behave. Miss Brady was by the entrance as mum wheeled me through the door. I quickly pulled away from Mum and pushed myself in. I didn't want anyone to see me being pushed by Mum. Miss Brady looked so different from the way she looks in school. She had on a pair of jeans, trainers and a checked shirt. She came over and welcomed me in, told mum what time to pick me up, and said, "Don't worry, I will look after her." As she said this, she looked down at me and gave me a wink. "We will make sure she has a good time, Mrs Duke."

The noise in there was deafening; there was a decent sound system and people were putting different music on. We went into a large room which had a couple of pool tables, a table tennis table, footballs and goals, and lots of chairs. There were some old-looking musical instruments piled in one corner of the room. The kids were all in small groups of mainly just girls or just boys. I recognised a few from school, but even though I could feel everyone staring at me, no-one spoke to me at first. I tried not to make eye contact with anyone, to avoid anyone saying anything nasty to me.

"So, there's lots going on here –
loads to choose from. Come in here;
this is another room where you can
sit and do art work or write stories
or poems," explained Miss Brady.
"We have a small library, too, if you
just want time out to sit and read."
I laughed and said, "as if."
"Listen, you're not in school now.
Don't tell anyone else, but in here
you can call me Kim. I trust you,
okay? But be careful in school,
okay?".
I think I actually blushed when she
said this. I went over towards the
sound system and said hi to a few
girls who were okay, and then had a
look at the CDs they had brought
in. When this was happening I

thought about what Kim had said –
how she seems to like and
understand me and how much all
the bullying and stress of losing dad
has affected me and turned me
into someone I don't know
anymore. Why am I hurting myself?
And why am I starving myself on
purpose? I am getting so tired all
the time, from not eating. These
girls at youth club, and Laura and
the Goths, are so confident and
popular, with loads of friends. I
want to be like that but I know
that being the way I am, the goody
two-shoes pupil, just isn't going to
get me anywhere. I hate Mum
calling me Charlotte, as well. She
usually calls me that if I am in

trouble. Seizing the opportunity, I announced to Kim, "From now on I want to be called Charlie. It's much cooler, I think. Will you call me Charlie?"

"Yeah, okay. Hi Charlie! Well, enjoy yourself tonight, and if you need anything just come and find me, okay?"

For some reason I was drawn to go back into the art room. I don't have the first clue how to draw or paint but I wanted to see what people had done. I went in and saw paintings and sketches on the tables, and sculptures and photos on the wall from when artists had done projects with the group. It looked like they had a great time. I came across a book called 'My Thoughts and Feelings.' Inside the first page there was something written: "What goes in this book stays in this book." I looked further through the book and found a page called 'My Battle isn't Over', written by Kim Brady. It was like a diary entry of her feelings and how she is coping after being in the Army. I couldn't believe what I was reading; it was so sad and full of details of what she went through. I felt a tear trickle down my cheek as I read it to the end. I found a place at the table and picked up a pen. Before I knew what was happening I began to write some words:

I look out the window what do I see? a broken heart looking back at me. Shattered with torment, trapped by fear, frightened no one's gonna find me. But when you find me will you look the other way? Or will you hold me? Promise me you will stay. Just like the others you will sleep for a while in my arms like an infant. The moment the sun rise breaks your dreams, you'll be gone in an instant, and I will keep on searching through the darkness of my mind ,stranded here in loneliness as love leaves me behind. Save me, love, don't leave me like this.

I don't know where this came from but there it was, staring me in the

face. I read it back and gave myself
a little smile; it was actually quite
good, for me, the one who they say
won't pass any exams or do
anything good at school. I closed
the book and just as I was about to
move from the table the door
opened and in walked Kim. I wasn't
expecting her to walk in and was a
bit embarrassed. She asked me
what I was doing and I said,
"Nothing, just having a look at the
artwork and photos." I pushed the
book further away and quickly
wheeled passed her and back into
the main room. There was a new
lady in the room when I went back,
standing by the kitchen drinking a
coffee. She was wearing a leather

jacket and leather trousers and held a motorbike helmet under one arm. I couldn't help notice how tanned her skin looked, and she had jet black, short spiky hair. She wasn't very tall but looked like she might be quite strong. Maybe she goes to the gym? I sat opposite her for a while and bought a can of Coke to drink. Kim came out of the art room and walked over to the new lady and they chatted for a while, laughing a lot.

I couldn't believe how quickly the night had gone; it was soon time for Mum to pick me up. Everyone began to leave. Parents arrived and left, but mum was late, as usual, and I was the last kid there. Kim talked to me as she was packing things away, and introduced me to the other lady. She told me her name was Cat. It wasn't her real name, she said. She was from the Netherlands and her real name was Caterina -"too long and hard for us Brits to say, so I christened her Cat." Kim seemed to enjoy telling me this, and laughed out loud as she did so. Then she knelt down beside my wheelchair and said, quietly, "I saw what you wrote in the book earlier. It's really good." Just as Cat was about to leave, they walked away from me so I couldn't hear properly, but I think they had an argument because Cat left soon afterwards, storming out

of the room and slamming the door.
I heard her start up her motorbike,
which was loud, and she seemed to
speed off very fast.

"She's a maniac on that thing. I
keep telling her to slow down," spat
Kim. I asked how they knew each
other and Kim explained that they
served together in Bosnia. Cat was
working for the UN forces, in
Intelligence, and when they both
left she came to live with Kim.
Mum eventually arrived in a fluster,
and we left. As I said goodbye to
Kim she looked really upset – so
different from the confident Miss
Brady in school.

"See you for P.E., Miss," I said, as we
walked out of the door, but there

was no reply. I wanted to rush back in and put my arms around her and ask if she was okay, but she wouldn't like that because, well, I'm just a kid! But I'm very worried. She might tell me more tomorrow, so I don't have to wait long.

Friday April 29th

Hiya, Silent One. We had some people in school this morning, talking about careers and colleges and universities, and there were a couple from the armed forces. Guess who was there from the Army? Cat! She's now working for the army careers department, talking in schools and events to promote the work the army does, and the jobs available. Funny Thing: I was in the playground after for break and I saw her walk to her bike with Kim following closely behind. They were arguing, I think, but I couldn't hear, as I was trying to hide from them. The funny thing was that, just as she got on her bike, Cat leaned over and gave Kim a long kiss... I couldn't believe it – my Kim is a lesbian, but she has a girlfriend... gutted! But if they are arguing a lot maybe they will split up soon. This is huge gossip. If Laura and the others found out, Kim would be in so much trouble, I think. Should I tell Emily? I just don't know if I can keep this secret to myself. What shall I do? I had

P.E. last lesson, with Kim. She seemed very quiet - didn't crack any jokes and was quite impatient with me. I asked her what was wrong and she just snapped back at me: "I'm fine, thank you. Now do ten more." I was doing work with the gym ball.

Just as I was leaving the lesson she reached in her bag for her phone and started to look at it. She looked angry and threw it back inside her bag, quickly picked up her trainers and left the room, leaving me to tie my own laces and leave. She always ties my laces - we always laugh at the size of my tiny feet - so why didn't she stay today and do this? I bet she has fallen out with

Cat again. It is making Kim so
unhappy; I hate the idea of her
being sad.

Thursday May 5th

Today was a bit of a mix. I went back to youth club, after twisting Mum's arm, and a few of the girls started chatting to me around the music system. They showed me a few of their CDs and Megan even said she would burn a CD for me, which is great. A lot of the older girls seem to like weird stuff. They dress in black and have black make up and nails. They like bands like The Cure and The Smiths and Echo and the Bunnymen, most of which I hadn't heard of. I quite like The Smiths, though; the lead singer has a really cool hairstyle.

Kim wasn't in school or at club tonight, either. I was told she is away on a course this week. I know she had a bad cold on Friday, too. I hope she's okay. I am actually getting on with a couple of the boys at Youth Club. That didn't go down well with Mum when I told her.

"Boys that age only want one thing. You just look after yourself and be careful who you trust, lady," she repeated at least three times over tea tonight.

But I'm not worried. They were great fun. They kept asking to take it in turns to push me around the car park really fast. It was a bit scary, but they enjoyed it, and, well... I did too! Cat was there, helping out, and just said that Kim was "fine" when I asked her. I still think they are not getting on, and it makes me wonder if Cat is cheating on her. I hope she isn't: I will kill her if I find out she is. Anyway, the boys tried to get me involved with their ball games tonight. I got brave and got out of my chair, much to Dave's horror. Dave is the other Youth Leader. He is a bit older - grey hair, big belly, but is always whistling and singing to himself. He reminds me of Dad for some reason; I think he even wears the same aftershave. I think he has a soft spot for me: he started calling me Treacle, in his broad Cockney accent, which was so funny to hear in such a rural place. London is miles away; I wonder why he is living here?

I miss having a dad around. Mum is trying her best, but who can I talk to about football? Dad was always taking me to matches and telling me how good "his" team (West Ham United) are. I also miss all the fun we had down in the garage, when they had the business. He would give me little jobs to do, like sanding down panels so they could be resprayed. I would help out with washing the cars, too, as best I could. He would take me over to the big barrel of oil cleaner, to wash my hands before leaving. It was weird stuff, green in colour and very slimy, with a very unusual smell, but it was like magic. Dad would finish work – his hands totally black in oil and dirt – then, after washing in this stuff, his hands would look perfectly clean. I loved the smell, too. I never did find out what it was called... guess I never will. I was always a tomboy as a small kid. Mum did dress me up in girls' clothes as best she could, but as soon as I was old enough I stopped that. She would say to me, often, "You look like a little boy," so, of course, now I'm dressing myself, this is exactly the look I'm going for. I did some research and I like the way lesbians seem to dress - very comfortable, too. Jeans, mostly, which is much better than skirts. I hate my uniform at school. Everyone can see my skinny, horrible legs, and make fun all the time.

One of my friends from the village came to see me after school. He was all excited. He always brings me new and exciting music to listen to. He is a bit older than me, but he is very cool and we get on well.

He said, "You have to listen to this singer; she's got a fantastic voice and I think she's a lesbian."

I had spoken to him, briefly, asking him questions about lesbians, which is why he mentioned this. I looked at the picture on the CD cover and my eyes almost popped out of their sockets. At first I thought it was a man, then I looked closer and she was really good looking and I *loved* what she was wearing. We listened to the CD and I *loved* it, so after he left I asked mum if I could go on the computer we have just had. I'm not too good on it yet, but we are learning at school. I went on the Internet and looked up this mysterious singer for information, and there it was – confirmation that she was a lesbian: 'Kd Lang, lesbian singer from Canada', it said. BOOM! There it was in black and white – my new idol. She is gorgeous and so talented. I left the living room after switching off the computer, and took down all the other posters I had in my bedroom. It is time to grow up and like better music and she is going to be the one I look up to from now on.

P.S. Instead of gossiping about me in school, everyone is making up stories about Kim and saying she's in hospital. I know she's just on a course, so why would they make up such stories?

Thursday May 5th

I HATE school! I found out it was Laura's birthday and gave her a card today, and everyone kept teasing me and her afterwards, saying I fancy her and that we are lovers kissing behind the bike sheds, and all that rubbish. At first, Laura thought it was funny, then she got really mad. I heard them sniggering

and talking about me at break,
saying stuff like: "So, you think
rubber legs is a lesbian, then?" and,
"So, someone's got a girl crush on our
Laura! Are you going to snog her
face off, Lau?" When I went
through the door of our form room, I
had to move the bin because it had
fallen over. When I put it back, I
saw the card I gave Laura, ripped
up and stuffed in the bin... I am SO
angry!

I heard some of the teachers
talking about Kim, at lunchtime,
and they mentioned the name of
the hospital she's in... so it's true,
then. I'm worried that if she's in
hospital it must be serious.

Emily is meeting me in town on Saturday. Mum is dropping me off. We are going shopping and getting a McDonald's. I thought I might get Kim a get well card and take it to the hospital. Emily didn't like the idea at first, but it's not far to go. We are getting one of those buses that have floors that lower for wheelchairs and push chairs to get on. I've never been on a bus; I'm not sure if I'm scared or excited, but I have to see Kim. I've stopped eating again since I heard about her being in hospital, I'm so worried. I'm not telling Mum; she wouldn't like it and wouldn't let me go out if I told her, so I hope no one sees me in town.

Wednesday May 11th

I can't believe what happened in school today. Emily was all nervous and giggling and said she had to tell me a big secret, which, at first, I was happy about. She said she really liked someone in school, A LOT, like – can't stop thinking about them – but couldn't do anything about it. She wouldn't say who it is, but said, "You know them very well." We have sorted out our plan for Saturday: we are meeting in McDonald's at 11am and going on from there. If she gets a boyfriend she won't want to hang around with me at school, so I hope the boy doesn't like her back. I know that's bad to say, but I will have no one if she disappears.

Wednesday May 11th

My head is a mess. I cannot believe what happened on Saturday! I need to talk about it to someone, but I'm trying to get my head around it as well. First of all, we were walking through the park to go feed the ducks when Emily started to get all serious and said she had something important to tell me.

She said she couldn't keep it from me any longer and she knelt down next to me by the lake and kissed me ON THE LIPS! She told me that she had feelings for me she didn't fully understand. I was a bit shocked at first, but after she kept touching me on the shoulder or trying to hug me and I actually quite liked it. She is pretty. Anyway, before I knew what was happening we were hiding behind a statue in the park and kissing, like... proper kissing, and stopping now and again to giggle. We bumped noses a lot and at one point I accidentally bit her lip, making it bleed a bit, which I felt bad about, but she said it didn't matter. I have no idea what will happen now, but it happened and it felt / feels nice. She is lovely, but what about Kim? I know I'm loads younger, but I can't get her out of my head, especially now I've seen where she is.

We went to Reception at the hospital and asked for directions to the Willow Ward, which is where we heard the teachers say she was.

"Are you sure that's where you want to get to?" asked the receptionist, looking puzzled.

"Yes, we are sure," I declared. "We are visiting someone there."

We got directions and went in the lift to the third floor. Along the corridor there were signs for 'Counselling Outpatients' and

'Psychiatric Admissions'. Finally, we found a door labelled Willow Ward.

"How can I help you, ladies?" asked a very scary looking nurse.

"We are here to visit our teacher, Miss O'Hara," said Emily.

"She means Kim, Kim O'Hara. We are here to see Kim O'Hara; we have a get well card for her," I said.

The nurse looked us up and down, but told us to wait there whilst she checked with someone. She came back about ten minutes later and said that we were not allowed to see Kim, as we were not on her visitors list, whatever that means. But I insisted – "We have come all this way; we just want to see her

for five minutes. It's really important we see her, please miss, just five minutes, then we will leave."
She disappeared again and eventually returned with a smile on her face.

"I've spoken to Kim; she's very surprised to hear you are here, but she said okay, just for five minutes. Don't make too much noise. If my boss found out I let in a couple of children I would be shot."

We agreed to be good and she showed us in to a large room with a TV, tables and chairs, and a trolley loaded with tea cups and snacks. Some people were slumped in their chairs, asleep; some people were walking about, shouting nonsense, and some people were chatting to each other. We found Kim in a quiet corner by the large window, which overlooked beautiful gardens.

"Hello Kim, how are you?" I said, as we approached her. She looked up and seemed embarrassed.

Emily offered the card and said, "We bought you a get well card, Miss, ' hope you like it."

We sat next to her quietly, not sure what to say.

"You shouldn't be here. Charlie, does your mum know you're here?"

"No," I replied, expecting to be shouted at.

"I suppose I better tell you why I'm here, then. I'm not very well, but not in my body, in my head, you see.

The doctors talk to me, sometimes
on my own and sometimes in
groups."
I couldn't believe it; this was a
mental health unit. I finally worked
it out.
"Is it that thing you said to me, the
PTSD thing, Miss?" I looked down,
waiting for the reply.
"Yes, Charlie, it is PTSD. I'm not
coping well. It's been very bad
recently, so bad that Cat has
moved out. So I need some help, but
you mustn't tell anyone at school,
okay? I will be back in a few weeks
if all goes well."
"Is Cat your girlfriend, Kim?" I was
nervous about asking this, but Kim
had tears in her eyes as she replied:

"See, I knew you were a smart cookie, Charlie; yes, she was, but isn't now. She's moved out - can't cope with my moods and behaviour. That's why I'm in here to get help."

After ten minutes, the nurse came over and said we had better leave or she would get into trouble.

"Please, nurse, can I come to see Kim again?" I blurted.

She looked over at Kim.

"If it's okay with you, nurse, yes, I'd like that. But you have to come with your mum, next time. Tell her, okay? I don't want you getting into trouble."

I agreed and turned to leave. When Emily put her arm around me I didn't like that: I didn't want Kim

to see; I don't know why - I quickly
moved away.

"See you again, Kim," I said.

"Thanks for coming, love birds." She
was smiling. "I don't miss a trick. I
might be unwell, but I'm not blind."
Kim laughed and picked up the
paper from the table next to her.

"Bye, Kim. Take care." ♡

I can't believe, for one thing, she is
in a mental unit, and for another,
she saw something between Emily
and me! So there it is, Silent One; it
seems that I have a girlfriend. How
am I going to explain *that* to Mum?
Can I keep it secret? I wonder
what she would say? Dad would
probably say something funny, but
I think he would be okay. I miss him

so much at the moment – wish I could speak to him or get a cuddle from him; he gave the best cuddles.

Wednesday May 25th

Hello, Silent One. Sorry for not writing much, but I've been busy with school assignments and I've been having so much fun at Youth Club. Emily comes with me, now. The others are okay, but I think they are still getting used to me. The youth worker, Dave, has been really sweet and he presented me with a ramp he made by hand, which means I can get up onto the main stage. We have a talent show next week and I'm singing a song, so I need to get onto the stage. I wasn't going to do it but Emily persuaded me. She said, "You have such a lovely voice, why shouldn't you have a go?" But I think she is just being nice. She's so sweet and keeps leaving me notes in my exercise books and giving me those love heart sweets. She is the only person in school who really understands me. Kim is still in hospital. I still can't stop thinking about her. She looks so great and is good to me, but I know she wouldn't be interested. I spoke to Cat, who is helping out at Youth Club until Kim comes back. She doesn't speak to the kids much - does a lot of the lifting of equipment and cleaning the rooms. She seems sad, I think she misses Kim. She was washing up in the kitchen and when she rolled up her sleeves I saw she has a lot of tattoos. She has a 'K' on her wrist... I asked her if she had spoken to Kim and after a pause she said: "Yes, briefly, on the phone. She's doing much better and they might let her home next week. She's seeing the doctor on Monday, so I said I would phone her Monday lunchtime."

I've no idea when she will be back in school, but I did ask Cat to give her my love when she speaks to her next, which she reluctantly agreed to.

Mum has asked me to go away with her and my little sister, Dylan, for a few days during half term; we don't have much money so it won't be abroad. She is looking at holiday parks to go to. She knows Emily and I are "best friends", so asked if I would like her to come with us. I'm so excited about that! Emily said she would go with me to see Kim again, on Saturday. I'm not sure if we will be allowed a second time, but we are going to try. If she goes home, then I definitely won't be able to see her, so this is my only chance. I think Emily is confused

about why I want to see her again;
I just explained that she's the only
teacher I trust in school and that
want to tell her how well I'm doing
with school work and the exercises
she gave me in class. I think Emily
believes me... for now. It's hopeless;
I finally understand my feelings: I
have a girlfriend but I'm so hung up
on Kim: she's gorgeous, funny,
smart, and really encourages me to
do well. She's *amazing!* Am I in
love? If this is what being in love
with someone you can't have, is like,
then I'd rather not be. Emily is
great, but she's not Kim! I've
stopped eating again: better hide it
well this time. I might start wearing
bigger tops to hide the fact I'm

losing weight. It seems that when I get upset or worried I lose my spirit and stop eating. What am I going to do? I'm going to get caught one day. Mum might hear me being sick or anything. I'm so worried, but I can't seem to stop this. We have exams in a couple of weeks, so I'm trying to revise lots, but I'm having trouble remembering things. I'm reading the books, but my memory is awful. Laura and the others think I'm thick because I sometimes have private lessons. It's only because those subjects are in rooms upstairs, where I can't get to, but they say I'm getting 'special treatment'. One of them even shouted to me as I went into the unit yesterday: "If you're that thick, why don't you go back to SPECIAL School?" and laughed as she past me in the doorway. Everyone else sniggered along with her. I hate School. Why can't Kim come back? Anyway, I've decided I'm only talking to Emily, now, in school. I'm studying hard - I will even ask for more help if I need to. And I *will* pass my exams, or at least do better than everyone expects. I just wish Kim could be there to help me; I'm sure she would be a great support teacher. The one I've got is okay but a bit stuffy and old; I can't really have a laugh with her like I'm always doing with Kim.

Thursday May 26th

I went to the staff room today, to see my form tutor. I wanted to ask if it would be possible to get any more help with revising. He said he knew I was able to get a time extension for my exams, but wasn't sure if more help within lessons was possible. I might have to do extra after school, when the rest are in detention, which means Laura will be around most of the time, as she seems to get detention at least once a week. I was told there will be a meeting and someone will talk to me as soon as there is any news.

I heard the supply P.E. teacher say she is leaving on Friday, so I hoped that meant Kim would be coming back...

"Your favourite, Miss Hara, will be back after half term, Charlotte, so no more taking it easy in P.E., okay?" laughed Mr Ashley, as I past the doorway to the staff room, where he stood drinking his coffee. I had to try really hard to keep in the screech of "Yeahhhh!"

It's half term and Mum has booked us a holiday at Butlins. We are going on Monday, on the train, because mum can't fit my chair and all our luggage in her small car. We will have extra luggage because Emily is coming with us, which will be amazing. We are sharing a room so we get to hang out and snuggle up watching T.V. together, and Mum won't bat an eyelid. It's what girls do with their friends, right? I've decided to try not to get too excited about Kim, or think about her when we are away. I need to enjoy being with Em. She's perfect in so many ways, and is always telling me how amazing I am. We have bought a load of new music – The Smiths and

The Cure. Mum isn't too impressed: she says it's just a noise and sounds like they are singing in pain most of the time. I'm trying to get Em to like Kd Lang, too. She says she's a bit weird, but I think she's just very quirky and unique. I listen to her songs on my headphones in bed each night, and dream about what it would be like to be friends with her. I bet she's a really good friend. She seems very kind and has the nicest smile... well, Kim has the nicest smile, but I must stop thinking about her.

Sunday May 29th

She's coming back, Silent One! I
know I shouldn't be so excited, but I
can't help it. We decided not to go
to see her again on Saturday.
Instead, Em and I stayed at home.
Mum trusted us enough to leave us
at the house whilst she went out for
the day with my aunties. We made
pizza and popcorn, and listened to

music, and just had a lovely time together, alone. We lay on the bed together, in a big cuddle, listening to music. which was so nice. I was naughty and kept tickling Em, making her squeal and myself laugh so much. We are so silly together, but it's nice and Mum still hasn't worked out what's really going on. A really lovely song came on the radio - Adele's "Someone Like You", and we just stopped messing around and lay there, eyes closed, holding each other. We almost fell asleep - that song is so beautiful. I know we have been listening to other stuff, like The Smiths, but I do like the soppy songs too. Em says she's going to download the album so we can listen to it whenever we like.

I can't wait for the holiday, now. We're picking up Em in a taxi, first thing, and heading off to the train station. Mum has had to ring up so many numbers to get us help on the train. She got really cross on the phone when the person gave her all the wrong information. I wish mum could afford a bigger car, then she wouldn't get stressed about us going anywhere.

I better go: I need to pack my things for our holiday, and get to sleep. I won't write anything when I'm away, but will have lots to report when I come home, I hope. This place better be good and we'd better have nice weather. There's loads to do there, mum said, and we can go to the entertainment at night. I just hope the disco plays some decent music. Good night Silent One, I'm hiding you under the mattress so mum doesn't find you when she cleans my room. I hope the food is good on holiday. I know I have been okay recently, but I'm worried that if I need to be sick after eating, I won't be able to, because either mum or Em will hear me. At least we will get some time alone; Mum says our room is next door to hers. There's a disabled room with two single beds and a room next door for Mum, so that means Em and I will share. Em says she wanted to 'do' lots of different things together, and I don't think she meant crazy golf! I'm actually quite scared by this idea. She says she has been looking things up on her computer, and reading books about lesbians. How she got hold of those, being under age, I don't know, but I'm not going to ask. I will tell you everything when I get back. I'm glad you're just a diary and won't shout at me when I write to you. Byeeeee, Silent One!

Sunday June 5th

What an amazing holiday, Silent One. I just don't know where to start.

The site was so easy to get around in my chair, and everyone there was so helpful. We had front row seats for the entertainment each night. I even got brave and sang in the talent contest on Wednesday.

I was shy, but Em said "Who cares? No one knows you here, and they won't see you again, will they?" She had a good point, so off I went to my room, chose my song and practised all day, Wednesday. Everyone performing was so good - lots of singers, comedians, a couple of dancers and me! They even lifted me, in my chair, onto the stage. I sang Madonna's 'Holiday' as I thought people would like that; and I came in fourth place, out of about ten acts, so I was very happy. Mum won a prize in the raffle that night, too, so she was very happy. I'm so happy with Em; we had the best time; we played loads of crazy golf, went swimming,

with Mum watching, just in case, as
I'm not a very strong swimmer.
Mum left us alone a lot in the day,
and we had dinner together and
watched the entertainment at
night. Em and I didn't do much
experimenting – we decided to take
things slow. We are happy as things
are, for now.

I'm so pleased Mum made some
friends at Butlins. She spent a lot of
the time with them and laughed a
lot. She hasn't laughed or smiled
much since the divorce, so going
away did us both good, I think. She
really likes Em, too; she says she
has seen a difference in me since
we became friends... wonder why?
Lol! I know sometimes mum shouts

and I feel she's being unfair with me, but it must be hard not having anyone else to help with me and Dylan. I think this holiday has bought us closer together. I do love her so much - maybe I should tell her more? Anyway, she's right, I am different - I feel happy. I know this thing with Kim is just a crush, but I like the fact she sees the real me and treats me how she does.

Monday June 6th

So, Kim's back! She says it's for a
couple of months' trial, as she's still
having some outpatient support.
She's not doing any teaching at the
moment, just catching up on
paperwork and having lots of
meetings. I spoke to her after break
and she said I took a risk coming to
see her in hospital and that she

hopes it didn't upset me too much...
bless her for thinking of my feelings.
Oh, wait, stop it, Charlie! It's just
nice having her back in school and
seeing her, even though she's not
doing any work with me. She did
say thank you for coming, though,
and winked at me. "I don't get any
other visitors, so it was nice to see a
friendly face." She asked if things
were okay with Em and me. I just
nodded and smiled.
She told me, today, that she is
getting lots of extra help and
support and will be back in Youth
Club in a couple of weeks. Cat has
moved away. Kim seems sad about
it, but says it's for the best for both
of them.

Tuesday June 7th

Silent One, this might be my last entry for a while, as I'm going to be busy! My teachers have said, in all my reports, that I am showing signs of really working hard this term. My grades are better and I'm beginning to work with my support teacher on ways to help me remember stuff. I'm getting extensions for all my written exams. I speak to the Goths when I have to, but I don't take any notice of their snide comments. I think they are annoyed I'm not bothered with them and their bullying. I'm not letting them spoil my education. I've decided I want to go to university when I'm older, so I have to study hard from now on. I want to help people with mental health problems, so I will need to study psychology and other really hard subjects. Mum thinks I'm crazy and should just go to college and learn computers and office work. If I could, I would love to be in the Air Force, but I don't think they would let in a kid in a wheelchair, would they?

I know the hospital doctors will continue to help Kim. She has a long way to go before she's better; she says she may not ever be totally cured, but understands her feelings better and knows where she can get help.

The final two years of school are ahead of me and I'm determined I'm going to prove everyone wrong. I did love my special school and loved my friends there, but in mainstream school I think I have learned so much more than I ever could at special school, and I'm not just talking about boring school subjects. By being here, I have really grown up and begun to know who I am, and what I want to do when I'm an adult. I have started to really understand about being lesbian and I think, even though I'm young, I do actually love Em. I know mum will struggle to understand this, but I know now, it's not her fault; she doesn't know any better or fully understand. She only knows what she hears and sees on TV.

I started writing this diary as a tiny scared caterpillar. I've had some really hard times, some scary, some sad and some lonely times, but there have also been some amazing times, and I think that tiny scared caterpillar is turning into a beautiful colourful butterfly

who is going to fly! Who knows, I
may even continue to write to you
sometimes, Silent One – I don't
think you have heard the last of me,
yet. Charlie Duke is happy, and
back on track, and there are a lot
more adventures to come... thank
you for listening.

Charlie

XOXOXOXOXO